Dedicated to my Baby Cousin Jianna

BEA

A Story on Social Distancing

Tomorrow is Bea's ninth birthday, yet she is not the least bit excited for the occasion.

A virus that is going around caused Bea's parents to cancel Bea's beach party.

Her parents explained that to stay healthy and help keep others healthy, they have to be social distancing.

"Bea, we need to try our best to stay inside and avoid going close to other people while the virus, a very bad germ, is still around. If we do go out it is our responsibility to wear masks and stay at least six feet away from people," Bea's mother told her.

Bea did not understand. *Virus? Social Distancing?* Bea and her parents were not sick. Her friends are not sick. Her grandparents are not sick. She did not understand why they could not all go to the beach tomorrow.

That night Bea did not speak to her parents and went straight to bed.

When Bea woke up, she found herself under a purple sky, and on top of clouds. As she looks around she sees people wrapped in blankets and appeared sluggish.

"Girl, where is your blanket? Without it, you may be **cursed**! Come take one from the basket.", said an Old Lady with blue hair.

Bea takes a blanket and asks what the Old Lady means by a curse.

The Old Lady explains to Bea that there is a monster, up North in Cloud Land's largest tree, who stole all the people's powers.

"He has cursed us if you do not wish to be cursed or curse anyone else you must stay apart from everyone you see. You have to wear the blanket, for it will protect you from losing your powers," the Old Lady firmly told.

Bea in disbelief asked, "Is there any way you can get your powers back?"

"I'm afraid that everyone who has tried has been cursed," the Old lady sighed.

Bea felt sorry that all the people lost their powers and decided she wanted to help: "I want to try!"

The Old Lady with blue hair felt Bea's sincerity, "You have a good heart. I will tell you. The monster, he is a **Prince**, but do not be fooled; he is the one who stole our powers. You must take his crown to end the curse."

"You can put your faith in me," Bea declared, and she went on her way to find the Prince.

On her journey to the Prince, Bea comes across a girl named Ameena weeping, so Bea stops to ask why the girl is upset.

Through tears, Ameena tells Bea, "I miss being with my friends. I miss having my powers. I wish things could go back to the way they were."

Bea felt her heart pang, like Ameena she wished she could see her friends and have a birthday party at the beach.

"Don't cry anymore Ameena, I will take the Prince's crown," Bea reassured.

On her journey to the Prince, a boy named Diallo piloting a plane flies by Bea.

It flies in loops and swoops back around right beside Bea, "Hey! There's nothing around these parts for miles, where do you need to go?",

Bea explained that she was heading to the Prince to end the curse.

Diallo's eyes could not hide his surprise, "You are a brave girl, hop on I will take you there".

As they cut through the air, Diallo tells Bea all about the curse and about the Prince.

"I'm still not sure I understand, how does coming close to people make me lose my powers?" Bea asked.

"The curse can spread from person to person. If you come near a person that has lost their powers, there is a big chance you too will become powerless," Diallo said.

Diallo continues, "It is strange though. I don't understand why the Prince has released this curse. He supported the people of Cloud Land's power."

Bea too did not understand why the Prince was acting so wicked towards his people.

Along the way, Bea and Diallo came across a group of people who were not swaddled in blankets. Diallo tells Bea there are some people on the Cloud Land that do not believe in the curse.

"There is **no** such thing as a crown stealing our power! Let us all gather around! We do not need blankets, they **do not** do anything!" The people with no blankets yelled.

Bea was shocked how the people did not believe in the curse.

Holding her blanket close to her skin, Bea told Diallo to lower the plane to speak out: "You need to stay apart from each other! Please wear your blankets, or more people will lose their powers!"

The people with no blankets stuck their tongues out and did not listen.

"It is no use, they will not listen. Let's focus on getting the Prince's crown to end the curse," said Diallo.

So Bea and Diallo continued to head towards the Prince.

Soon enough a towering tree came into view, with its long branches and rich green leaves.

Diallo lands the plane and they walk into the opening of the grand tree.

Finally, Bea and Diallo meet the Prince.

The Prince spoke first in an icy tone, "Do you two wish to be cursed as well?"

The Prince scared Bea, but when she thought back to all the people that lost their power- the Old Lady with blue hair, and Ameena who cried- Bea gathered her courage.

"Prince! All the people of the Cloud Land have lost their powers, you must take off your crown for them to get their powers back."

The Prince snickered and Diallo sensed something was wrong with the Prince.

The Prince no longer had kind eyes but cruel ones instead, and what most stood out to Diallo was the crown the Prince donned, it was black not gold.

Diallo spoke up, "Prince you are cursed!"

Just then a wizard appeared, "At last, Bea and Diallo! You two must come to help me if we are to save the Prince and the people of the Cloud Land from the curse."

The Wizard snapped his fingers and they were transported to the Wizard's tower.

The Wizard pulled out a scroll that read : "THE ANTI-CURSE SPRITZ FORMULA".

Altogether, the Wizard, Bea, and Diallo measured various spoonfuls and pinches of ingredients- aloe vera, glycerin, ethanol- words that reminded Bea of her hand sanitizer to make the spritz.

"Now mix! For the spritz to be potent, you two must put your heart into it. Think of all the people you wish to save." The Wizard said.

Once they were finished, the group of three smiled with glee.

The Wizard told Bea and Diallo the plan for when they met the Prince, then the Wizard snapped to once more meet the cursed Prince, but now with the spritz.

When they returned the three did not give the Prince a second to act, The Wizard and Diallo were already pinning his arms, and Bea doused the Prince with the spritz.

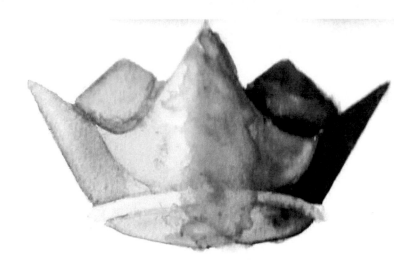

Slowly the black crown turned gold, and the Prince returned to normal.

Once they explained to the Prince the events that happened, the Prince spoke again, "A thousand thank yous to you three. Bea, I believe this belongs to you".

The Prince takes off his crown and explains, "This crown holds immense power, when sunlight shines through it, the crown can end the curse. But for it to work the people of Cloud Land must stand six feet apart."

So, the Wizard, Diallo, and the Prince worked to get everyone in place. When they were done, the Prince signaled to Bea, and she lifted the Crown for the sun to shine through.
It was a beautiful sight, one by one every person began to look much stronger.

Seeing Ameena, the Old Lady, and everyone regain their powers made Bea smile and say "This is the best birthday gift!"

"Happy Birthday Bea!" Bea woke up to her parents wearing party hats and a virtual call from Grandpa and Grandma.

Bea is now nine years old and understands how important it is to social distance, wear masks, and most of all have the desire for others to stay healthy.

fin

Made in the USA
Monee, IL
25 August 2020